This edition published by Parragon Books Ltd in 2015 and distributed by

Parragon Inc.
440 Park Avenue South, 13th Floor
New York, NY 10016
www.parragon.com

ISBN 978-1-4723-9639-6
Printed in China

Disney
MINNIE
A Splashing Date

Read the story, then turn the book over
to read another story!

Bath · New York · Cologne · Melbourne · Delhi
Hong Kong · Shenzhen · Singapore · Amsterdam

One lovely summer day, Mickey Mouse asked his girlfriend, Minnie, if she'd like to go for a boat ride.

"I would love to,"
Minnie said with a smile.
"A nice, easy float on the
lake sounds like the perfect
way to spend the day."

Mickey and Minnie were preparing to set sail
when Goofy came running by.

"Hiya, Mickey. Hiya, Minnie," he said and waved.
"What a great day for a boat ride!"

Goofy was looking at Mickey's boat and didn't see a
squirrel crossing his path. He accidentally stepped on its tail.

The squirrel leaped away and landed in the boat.

Mickey and Minnie were so startled that they jumped up, making the boat rock.

Mickey tried to stop the rocking, but he could not. The boat tipped over, sending Mickey and Minnie into the water!

Luckily, Donald Duck was
nearby in his speedboat and
saw what had happened.

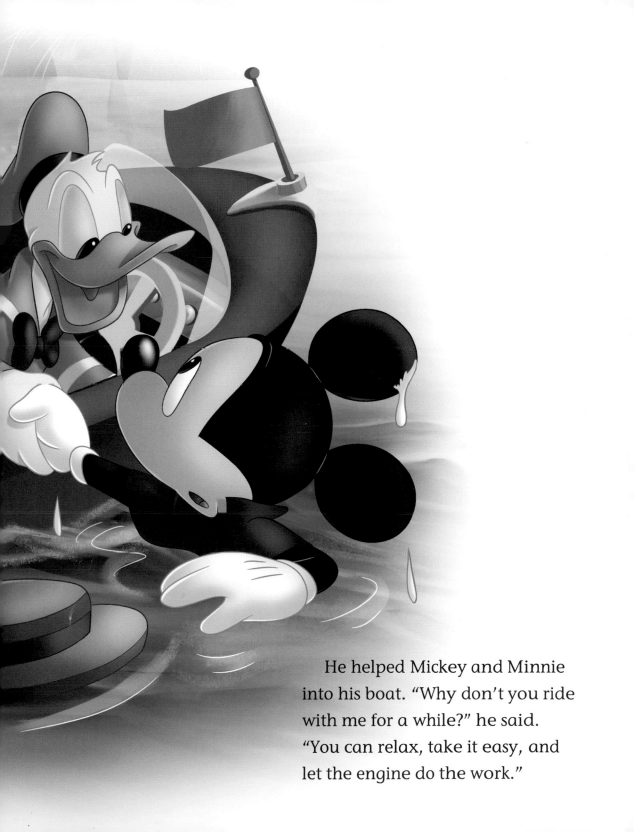

He helped Mickey and Minnie
into his boat. "Why don't you ride
with me for a while?" he said.
"You can relax, take it easy, and
let the engine do the work."

Mickey and Minnie sat back and relaxed. They had just reached the middle of the lake when the boat's engine suddenly stopped.

"Oh, no! What do we do now?" Minnie asked.

"I have an idea," Donald said. He took off his hat and started to paddle with it.

Mickey and Minnie did the same. Huffing and puffing, they made their way back to shore.

"How about some lunch while we dry off?" Mickey said.

Minnie agreed, and the two were soon relaxing in the sun with hot dogs.

As they were enjoying their lunch, Pluto came running past. When he saw the delicious hot dogs, he decided he wanted one, too. He jumped into Mickey's lap and tried to grab the food!

"Stop it, boy!" cried Mickey.

"Pluto," said Minnie, "if you want a hot dog, we can get you one."

But it was too late. Pluto knocked Mickey and Minnie right into the water!

Poor Mickey and Minnie climbed out of the
lake and settled on the grass to dry off again.
Soon, Donald Duck's nephews, Huey, Dewey,
and Louie, came by in their sailboat.

"Hey, Mickey," called Dewey. "Would you and
Minnie like to borrow our boat and go sailing?
There's a good wind today."

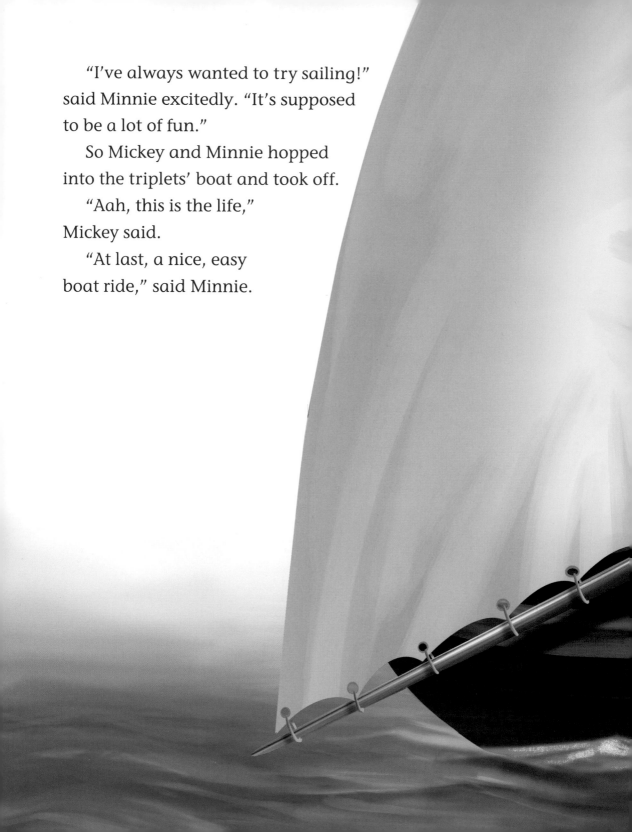

"I've always wanted to try sailing!" said Minnie excitedly. "It's supposed to be a lot of fun."

So Mickey and Minnie hopped into the triplets' boat and took off.

"Aah, this is the life," Mickey said.

"At last, a nice, easy boat ride," said Minnie.

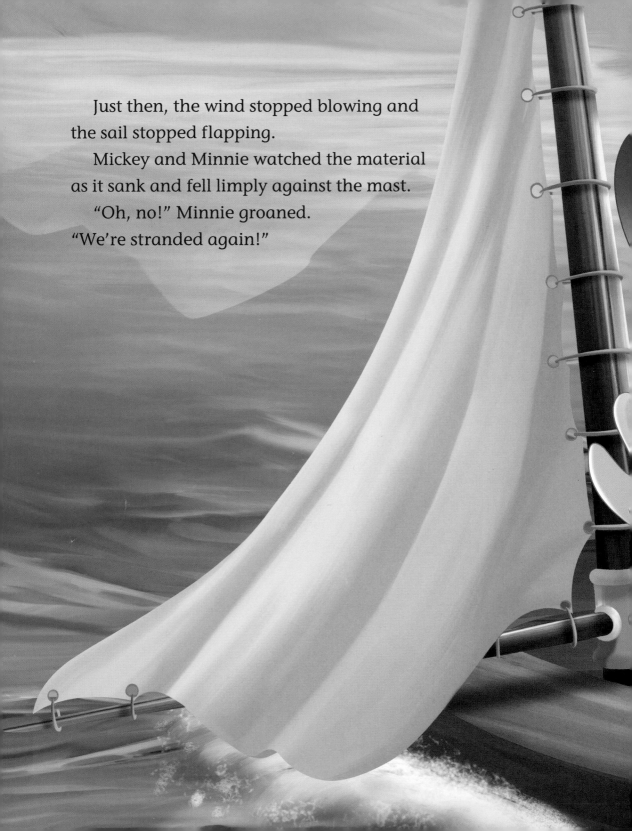

Just then, the wind stopped blowing and the sail stopped flapping.

Mickey and Minnie watched the material as it sank and fell limply against the mast.

"Oh, no!" Minnie groaned. "We're stranded again!"

Mickey and Minnie tried to paddle with their hands, but it was no use. They kept going round in circles.

Suddenly, Mickey looked up. Goofy and Donald were coming toward them in rowboats.

"We thought you might need some help," said Donald. He and Goofy attached a rope to the sailboat and towed Mickey and Minnie across the lake.

The happy couple didn't have to do a thing!

As the sun began to set over the peaceful lake, Mickey and Minnie sat back and relaxed. They had *finally* managed to have a nice, easy boat ride!

The End

Now turn the book over
for another classic Disney tale!

Now turn the book over
for another classic Disney tale!

The End

Finally, it really was time to leave.
Minnie and her friends packed their bags
and got into the car.

"That was so much fun!" said Donald as
they drove home. "Let's do it again tomorrow!"

As the sun set and the day started to get cooler, Minnie and her friends got out of the water.

Minnie had one last surprise for her friends . . . s'mores!

"Gee, Minnie," said Mickey, as they roasted marshmallows over a campfire, "you really do know how to plan the perfect summer day!"

"Aah," said Donald. "You were right, Minnie. This was a good idea!"

Minnie smiled to herself. She was glad she and her friends had found a way to cool off.

"I could stay in this water all day!" Daisy said.

And that is just what they did.

Donald really did want to go fishing, but finally he agreed to wait so all the friends could do something together first. After all, they *had* come to the lake to go swimming.

The friends put away their toys, changed into their bathing suits, and jumped into the water. . . .

Donald was about
to hop into the boat when
Minnie called out to him. "Wait up,
Donald," she said. "I don't think we can all
fit in the boat. Let's do something together!"
"But the water looks so nice!" said Donald.
"Why don't we go for a swim?" said Minnie. "We can *all* do that!"

Daisy wanted to play basketball.
Mickey and Pluto wanted to play fetch.
And Donald wanted to go fishing!
   Before anyone could stop him,
Donald raced off toward a little
boat docked beside the water.

When they arrived, everyone changed into their swimwear, ready for some splashing fun!

"Oh, it's so lovely and cool!" Mickey said happily.

"What should we do first?" Minnie asked.

Everyone had a different idea.

In no time at all, the friends were on their way. Pluto howled with glee as Mickey drove along the highway. They were so excited for their day at the lake!

Meanwhile, Minnie quickly threw her bathing
suit and a towel into her bag, as well as a little
treat for later. . . .

When everyone was ready, they headed back
to Mickey's house.

Daisy and Donald had been put in charge of the
food. Donald made stacks of sandwiches for everyone,
while Daisy packed bananas to share with her friends.

While Goofy was busy making a new batch of
lemonade, Mickey packed some tasty treats for Pluto.
"These should stop you from feeling hungry, boy,"
Mickey told Pluto. "Plus, you'll have fun chasing them!"

When he got home, Goofy made some more cool
lemonade for everyone. He also made quite a mess!
"Oh, yummy!" he said as he tried the lemonade.
He drank some more. And then some more. Before
long, all the lemonade was gone! "Uh-oh, guess I'd
better make some more," said Goofy.

Suddenly feeling excited, the friends raced home to pack.
Goofy asked Mickey and Pluto to come to his house to
help him get ready.

"Gosh, that breeze sure feels good!" Goofy said as the
friends skipped through the park. "But I can't wait to
totally cool off at the lake!"

"I've got an idea!" Minnie began, excitedly. "Let's go to the lake! There's always a breeze there, and there's so much to do!"

"What a great idea!" said Mickey.

"It's the perfect day for a swim," Daisy added.

Startled by Minnie's shout, everyone else jumped up, too!
"What is it, Minnie?" asked Mickey.

As Minnie watched her friends looking at the sprinklers, she suddenly had an idea. "I've got it!" she shouted, as she jumped out of her chair.

"Gosh, those sprinklers look nice and cool!" said Goofy, pointing down at Mickey's lawn.

Donald nodded. "But there isn't enough water coming out of them to keep *us* cool!" he said.

"Maybe we could make fans?" Minnie suggested.

"Or we could try sitting in the shade under the tree?"
said Mickey.

"Yes, or we could. . . ." Minnie's voice trailed off.
"Oh, it's too hot to think!"

"What are we going to do now?" asked Daisy, as she mopped her brow.

Minnie looked around. "Hmm. . . ," she said, using her magazine to fan her face. "We could make more of this delicious lemonade to keep us cool."

"But we'd have to do that in the house," Mickey groaned. "At least it's slightly cooler out here."

"Maybe there will be a breeze outside," said Minnie, hopefully. The group went out to the backyard . . . but there was no breeze. Just nice, cool lemonade from Mickey's refrigerator.

It was a hot summer day. Mickey Mouse and his friends were relaxing in his living room. The friends were just deciding what to do with their day when *pop!* Mickey's air conditioning broke!

DISNEP

MINNIE
A Summer Day

Read the story, then turn the book over
to read another story!

Bath · New York · Cologne · Melbourne · Delhi
Hong Kong · Shenzhen · Singapore · Amsterdam

This edition published by Parragon Books Ltd in 2015 and distributed by

Parragon Inc.
440 Park Avenue South, 13th Floor
New York, NY 10016
www.parragon.com

ISBN 978-1-4723-9639-6
Printed in China